The Case Of The

GAME SHOW MYSTERY

Look for more great books in
The New Adventures of
MARY-KATE & ASHLEY™

series:

The Case Of The
GAME SHOW MYSTERY

by Jim Thomas

■HarperEntertainment
An Imprint of HarperCollins*Publishers*

A PARACHUTE PRESS BOOK

PARACHUTE PRESS

Parachute Publishing, L.L.C.
156 Fifth Avenue
New York, NY 10010

DUALSTAR PUBLICATIONS

Dualstar Publications
c/o Thorne and Company
A Professional Law Corporation
1801 Century Park East
Los Angeles, CA 90067

HarperEntertainment

An Imprint of HarperCollins*Publishers*
10 East 53rd Street, New York, NY 10022

ISBN 0-06-106649-4

HarperCollins®, 🎬®, and HarperEntertainment™ are trademarks of
HarperCollins Publishers Inc.

First printing: January 2002

Printed in the United States of America

10 9 8 7 6 5 4 3 2 1

DOUBLE TROUBLE!

"**N**o! Wait! Don't do it!" Patty O'Leary shrieked. "Please! Don't slime me!"

"Sorry, Patty, but you know the rules," I said.

"A wrong answer means *it's slime time!*" my sister, Ashley, added.

"Noooooo!" Patty wailed.

I leaned over the game board and pressed a stamper to the back of Patty's hand. A mark that looked like a splat of green slime appeared there.

"Yuck! That's so gross!" Patty pouted.

Ashley and I were playing the home version of our favorite TV game show, *Double Trouble*, with our friends Patty O'Leary and Tim Park. Patty and Tim were on one team, and Ashley and I were on the other.

Our basset hound, Clue, was hanging out, too. The five of us were spread out on the living room floor in our house.

I picked up the dice from the board and handed them to Tim. "It's your turn," I told him. "Go ahead and roll."

Tim shook the dice in his fist. "Come on six!" he cheered. He dropped the dice on the board. He rolled a five. He frowned as he moved his game piece along the board. It landed in the "ask a question" space.

"Excellent!" Ashley cheered. She reached over to give Clue a scratch behind the ears. "We are so good at this part!"

Tim picked a game card from the deck in

front of him. I grabbed my pencil and paper.

In *Double Trouble*, one person on a team writes down an answer to the question, and the other person guesses what her teammate wrote.

Tim read out loud from the card. "What is your favorite color?"

I quickly scribbled something on the paper, then flipped it over so my answer was facedown.

Ashley smiled. "That's an easy one. Mary-Kate's favorite color is purple."

I grinned and flipped over my paper. I showed Patty and Tim what I'd written: PURPLE.

"You're right...*again*," Tim said in a bored voice. "That's ten more points for your team."

"Yay!" I cheered. I gave Ashley a high five. "Way to go!"

"But it's not fair!" Patty wailed. "You

guys are *twins*! You know everything about each other. Tim and I don't stand a chance!"

I smiled. I hated to admit it, but Patty was right. Ashley and I were a totally awesome *Double Trouble* team.

"When you go on the *Double Trouble* TV show, you're going to be the highest-scoring players in history!" Tim told us.

I grinned. "We're definitely going to do our best."

"I just wish I didn't feel so nervous," Ashley said.

"Me, too. I have about a jillion butterflies in my stomach," I admitted.

About a month ago, Ashley and I were shopping at the mall and one of the stores we visited was having a raffle. The grand prize was the chance to play *Double Trouble* on TV!

We bought two raffle tickets right away. But we couldn't believe it when the store called last week to tell us that we had won! Today was the day of our big TV debut.

Ashley checked her watch. "The TV people should have picked us up by now. You don't think they forgot about us, do you?"

"Forget about the famous Trenchcoat Twins? No way!" Patty laughed.

Ashley and I are kind of famous. We have our own detective agency in our attic. And together we are a lean, mean crime-solving machine.

Ding-dong! The doorbell chimed.

Ashley and I turned to each other. "It's them!" we said together.

Ashley rushed to the door and opened it wide. The rest of us crowded in behind her.

A beautiful blond woman in a suit stood facing us. "Hi, I'm Lauren," she said. "I'm with the game show *Double Trouble*. You must be the Olsens."

Ashley nodded. "That's right. I'm Ashley.

This is my sister, Mary-Kate." She pointed her thumb at me.

"It's nice to meet you." Lauren shook hands with both of us. "So—are you girls ready for your big TV appearance?" she asked.

"Absolutely!" I cheered. "We can't wait!"

"Great!" Lauren said. "Then let's go!"

She stepped to the side. Behind her, waiting for us at the curb, was the longest stretch limousine I'd ever seen!

"Whoa!" Tim gasped when he caught sight of the car. "Nice ride!"

"Yeah! It's almost as nice as the limo my dad hired for my birthday last year," Patty told us.

I rolled my eyes. To Patty, *everything* is a competition.

Tim hung his backpack over his shoulder. "See you later," he called as he stepped out the door. "Good luck!"

"I'm going to tell everyone I know that

my friends are on television!" Patty said. "Bye!" She followed Tim down the street.

Our mom and dad came to the door to greet Lauren. After Lauren gave my mom some papers to sign, we were ready to go. Ashley and I both hugged our mom and dad good-bye. Then we grabbed our backpacks and followed Lauren to the limo.

"We are so excited to be on the show," Ashley told Lauren.

"I have to admit," Lauren said, "I'm excited to meet you. I'm a big fan of yours."

"Really?" I asked.

"Uh-huh." Lauren nodded. "You two are the best detectives around. Everyone knows that the Trenchcoat Twins can solve any crime!"

Ashley and I smiled at each other. We *do* love solving mysteries. But today we weren't detectives—just contestants on our favorite game show!

Lauren opened the limo door for us, and

Ashley and I climbed in. It was *huge* inside! There was a TV against the back of the front seat and a big sunroof over our heads.

"Wow," I said. "This is so cool!"

"Yeah," Ashley said. "I feel like a movie star!"

Lauren smiled as she slid in behind us and closed the door. "Only the best for our contestants!" she said. Then she offered us a soda from a tiny refrigerator in the car.

Lauren told the driver to head to the studio. Slowly, the limo glided away from our house.

Lauren took a pair of eyeglasses and some papers from her briefcase. "Now, I'm supposed to go over the rules of the show with you—"

"Oh, you don't have to do that," Ashley interrupted. "We know the rules by heart! We watch the show all the time."

I nodded. "We never miss an episode."

"In that case, why don't you explain the

rules to me—just so I'm sure there's nothing that you're forgetting?" Lauren suggested.

"Well, each show has three parts," I started to explain. "The quiz, the obstacle course, and the scavenger hunt."

"During the quiz," Ashley continued, "four teams of brothers and sisters answer questions about each other. The contestants get points for right answers."

"But for wrong answers, *it's slime time*!" I cheered.

"And on TV, it's real slime—not just a stamp." Ashley made a disgusted face. "Yuck!"

I knew Ashley hated the idea of getting slimed. But in my opinion, sliming was one of the best things about the show! People always looked so funny dripping with green goo. And the goo they used looked totally gross. I couldn't wait to see if it felt as icky as it looked.

"You both have really good memories,"

Lauren said. "I'd hate to play against the two of you. You make a terrific team!"

Ashley and I glanced at each other. I knew what Ashley was thinking. Of course we make a great team. We're twins! The other contestants would never be able to beat us!

"Here we are!" Lauren called as the limo came to a stop.

I glanced out the window at a large gray building.

"No way. *This* is where you tape *Double Trouble*?" I asked.

Ashley seemed as surprised as I was. "The show is so exciting, with flashing lights and everything. But this building is really…plain."

"Yeah," I agreed. "I guess I expected a red carpet and a big sign or something."

Lauren laughed. "This is what most TV studios look like on the outside," she explained. "Don't worry. The set is inside and I'm sure that you'll recognize that."

The driver opened the car door for us, and we all climbed out. Lauren led us into the building.

Inside it was very dim. The ceiling was somewhere high above. Thick cables criss-crossed the floor. To me, they looked like long snakes.

"Creepy!" I whispered.

"No kidding," Ashley agreed.

"We need all this space for the lights and cameras," Lauren explained. "And keeping it dark makes it easier to light the set." She took a few steps ahead of us. "Come on, we're almost there."

But before we could follow, a tall man with a gleaming smile swooped toward us.

"Hello, ladies!" he called to us.

Ashley and I turned. "Drew Drewsdale!" we cried.

Drew Drewsdale is the host of *Double Trouble*. We are his biggest fans!

Drew shook our hands. "It's such a huge pleasure to have the Trenchcoat Twins on the show today."

"Thank you, Mr. Drewsdale," I said.

"Please," he said. "Call me Drew."

Ashley looked at me, and we both giggled. *Drew.* I thought. *How cool!*

Drew walked with us through the dark building. He talked a little about the show and how excited everyone was that we were going to be on it. I was so excited, I could barely pay attention to what he was saying!

"We're doing a special show today," Drew explained, "and it wouldn't be the same without you two."

That caught my attention. "Special show?" I asked.

"What do you mean, Drew?" Ashley asked.

Drew just smiled at us. "You'll see…"

We turned a corner and found ourselves at the edge of a brightly lit area. I recognized it right away. Ashley and I knew it almost as well as we knew our own living room. It was the set of *Double Trouble*!

"Wow!" Ashley said. "It looks amazing in person!"

"I can't believe we're actually here!" I agreed.

Four big desks—one for each pair of partners—were arranged in a semicircle on the set. Next to the desks was the obstacle course. It was huge! There were brightly colored barrels to crawl through and ropes to climb. There were ladders and ramps and slides. And all around the obstacles were pits filled with green slime!

It looked pretty difficult, but I wasn't worried. Ashley and I were going to be tough to beat! We had the twin advantage!

That's when I heard Ashley gasp. She grabbed my arm. "Mary-Kate, look!"

I turned to see what she was staring at. "Oh, no!" I cried. "I don't believe it!"

2

MEET YOUR OPPONENTS

"**T**wins!" I whispered.

Ashley and I stared at the other kids filing onto the set. When I saw them, I knew exactly what Drew had meant about a "special show."

"Today we'll be taping the very first twins edition of *Double Trouble!*" Drew grinned.

I groaned softly. It looked like Ashley and I weren't guaranteed to win after all.

"Olsens, follow me!" Drew said. "I'll

introduce you to all of the other players."

We stepped onto the set, and the group turned toward us. There were six other contestants in all. Each one was wearing a name tag.

"Everyone," Drew said, "meet Mary-Kate and Ashley Olsen, the Trenchcoat Twins!"

Ashley and I smiled at the group.

Drew motioned to a pair of boys. "This is Billy Branson and his brother, Bobby."

Billy smiled and waved, but Bobby just glared at us.

The Bransons were identical twins. They had the same hair color, the same eye color, and their faces were exactly the same.

It was easy to tell them apart, though. Billy wore glasses and had his hair slicked down and parted to the side. His glasses were held together in the middle with a piece of white tape. I cringed. It wasn't exactly the coolest look.

Especially for a TV show.

His brother, Bobby, had his hair styled into short spikes. And his clothes were really trendy. He wore a long T-shirt with big baggy pants. He didn't seem very friendly, though. He was the one glaring at us.

"Over there are Christina and Matthew Martinez," Drew continued. Christina and Matthew both smiled and waved at us. They looked a lot alike but weren't totally identical.

They must be fraternal twins, I thought, like Ashley and I.

Finally, Drew introduced the last pair of twins, Kathy and Marissa Goldbloom. When I looked at them, I had to blink twice.

Not only were Kathy and Marissa identical, they were *dressed* exactly alike! They looked like the mirror image of each other! Both wore frilly white dresses and shiny black shoes. If it weren't for their name tags, I wouldn't be able to tell them apart.

"Hi!" Ashley and I said.

The Goldblooms turned away from us without saying a word. Kathy was clutching a deck of small white cards. She held one card up at a time in front of Marissa. After each card, Marissa whispered something to Kathy.

I nudged my sister with my elbow. "What are they doing?" I whispered.

"Those look like flash cards," Ashley answered. "They must be quizzing each other!"

"Whoa!" I said. "Those girls are superserious about winning!"

Lauren walked up to us and attached *Double Trouble* name tags to our shirts. "Every contestant gets one," she explained.

"Why don't all you kids head back to the dressing room and get ready while I go into makeup," Drew suggested. He waved and headed off the set. "I'll see you in five minutes!"

"Okay, kids," Lauren called. "Follow me

to your home base—the dressing room."

Everyone picked up their bags. Lauren led the way to the backstage area. Like the rest of the building, it was dimly lit. The camera operators and other people who worked on the show were moving the cameras into place.

Soon we came to a row of doors. Lauren opened one labeled DRESSING ROOM and ushered us in. It was cozy inside, with couches and chairs. Along one wall there was a row of mirrors surrounded by round white lights. The Goldbloom girls immediately sat down in front of them and started fixing their hair, even though I thought they already looked perfect.

"I'll be back soon to call you to the set," Lauren said. "You kids get to know one another while I'm gone!"

Ashley and I dumped our backpacks in a corner of the room. Everyone else found a spot for theirs somewhere on the floor.

"So is this your favorite show, too?" someone asked us. I turned. Christina Martinez and her brother, Matthew, were standing next to us. They were both smiling.

"Are you kidding?" I answered. "Ashley and I never miss an episode."

"Neither do we," Matthew admitted. "I can't believe we're actually going to be on the show! I can't wait to get slimed!"

"Speak for yourself," Christina joked. "That slime looks really gross." She turned to us. "Hey, did you hear what the first prize is?"

Ashley and I shook our heads.

"A brand-new computer with a super-fast Internet connection," Matthew said. "Isn't that cool?"

"Matthew really loves surfing the Net," Christina explained. "He uses the computers at school as much as he can, but he thinks having one at home would be great."

"Come on! You know you want the computer, too. You're always over at your best friend Courtney's house using hers!" Matthew turned to us. "Christina hates to admit it, but she *loves* computer games."

Christina blushed. "Okay, okay, it's true. But have you guys ever played Starcraft? The graphics are so realistic! The way it works is—"

Matthew laughed. "See what I mean?" he said. "She's a total gamer!"

"Hey!" a boy's voice called. It was Bobby Branson. He and his brother walked over to us.

"Hi." Ashley smiled.

"I didn't come over to make friends," Bobby said. "I'm just here to warn you—I'm the star of my school's basketball team, and I play football and baseball, too. I know how to win, and I plan on winning today."

For a moment, Ashley and I just stood there with our mouths hanging open.

Was this kid *serious*? I wondered. Was

he actually trying to psych us out?

"Yeah, right." Christina snorted. "Thanks for the warning. But I think my brother and I are up for the challenge."

Bobby glared at her, then turned away.

Billy smiled at us shyly. "Ummm, hi," he said.

"Don't make friends with the competition!" his brother yelled at him. "Let's go, Billy."

"Sorry about my brother. He's kind of intense," Billy whispered to us. "Good luck!"

As he turned to go, he tripped. His glasses slid off his nose and cracked against the floor. The frames broke where they had been taped together at the bridge.

Bobby groaned. He picked up his brother's glasses. Then he took a roll of white tape from his shirt pocket and tossed it at Billy's chest. He shot us another hard stare.

"My brother may be a total klutz," Bobby said, "but don't get any ideas. We're still going to beat the pants off all of you today."

"Yeah, whatever," Matthew said.

Bobby walked across the room with his brother in tow.

"Man. What's his problem?" I asked.

"He's not the friendliest guy, is he?" Christina said.

"Definitely not," Ashley agreed. "What about those two?" She nodded her head at the Goldbloom sisters. Marissa was studying the flash cards. Her sister, Kathy, was fixing her hair with Shine 'n' Soft hair gel.

I cringed. Ashley and I tried a bottle of that gel once, but we had to throw it out. I *hated* the smell.

"So far, the Goldblooms have ignored everybody," Matthew told us. "They seem pretty focused on winning."

Ashley and I exchanged a nervous glance. We had no idea the competition at *Double Trouble* would be so fierce!

The door opened, and Lauren walked in.

"Okay, everyone!" she said. "Let's head out to the set. Taping is about to begin!"

"Ready to play?" I asked my sister.

Ashley pressed her lips together in a serious expression. "Yeah," she said. "Let's get out there and win!"

3

FOUL PLAY

I felt my heart thump with excitement. Everyone took a look in the mirror, then followed Lauren out the door.

The set was brightly lit now and bustling with activity. The camera and sound crews were running around, checking the cameras and microphones one last time.

"Good luck!" Christina called to us. She and Matthew sat down behind one of the four desks on the set. Ashley and I, and the rest of the kids, did the same.

Then Drew bounced onto the set. He took his place behind a desk across from us. "Time to begin," he called. "Are you ready?"

"Ready!" we all answered.

I grabbed Ashley's hand and gave it a squeeze for luck. She squeezed back.

A red light above one of the cameras clicked on. Drew smiled broadly into the camera and said, "Welcome to a special edition of *Double Trouble*! I'm your host, Drew Drewsdale. Today we don't just have brothers and sisters on the show. Today our contestants are all *twins*!"

Drew turned and welcomed all the contestants. When he got to us, he introduced us as the famous Trenchcoat Twins.

"I don't know about you," Drew said, beaming into the camera, "but everyone on the show is expecting great things from these sleuth sisters! They are the twins our other teams will have to beat today!"

Across the set, I could see the Bransons and Goldblooms staring hard at us. Even Christina and Matthew looked annoyed!

Thanks a lot, Drew, I thought. *Now everyone will want to gang up on us!* I could feel my face turning red with embarrassment.

After everyone was introduced, Drew started the first round of the show.

"As our viewers know, in the first round we'll send one person from each team backstage. Then we'll ask the remaining teammates questions about their sisters or brothers," Drew explained. "They'll write down their answers. Then we'll bring the teammates back and see how their answers match up. Right answers win points. Wrong answers mean..."

"It's slime time!" all the contestants shouted.

"That's right!" Drew said. "So let's play!"

Ashley and I had already decided that I'd be the one to go backstage. I stood up to leave the set. "Hey, good luck, Ashley," I whispered to her.

"No sweat," Ashley said. She gave me a thumbs-up.

I started backstage with Bobby Branson, Kathy Goldbloom, and Christina Martinez. Lauren led us back to the dressing room, where we couldn't hear what was happening on the set.

As soon as Lauren closed the door, Bobby stalked off to the other side of the room. I was about to say something to Christina when Kathy came up to me in her frilly dress and perfect hair. She gave me an icy look.

"I don't care if you *are* the Trenchcoat Twins," she said. "My sister and I have a foolproof plan. We're going to win, and there's nothing you can do about it."

I tried to ignore what she said. "Well, ummm, good luck," I told her.

Kathy tossed her hair and walked away.

She sat down in front of the mirror and started smoothing her dress. I checked Christina's reaction. She just shrugged.

We flopped down on one of the couches. Bobby was leaning in the corner, looking completely bored.

I kept thinking about Ashley. Out on the set, Drew was asking her and the other kids a bunch of questions. I tried to imagine what they might be. *What time does your sister or brother go to bed on school nights? What is your sister's or brother's favorite funny movie? What subject in school does your sister or brother like best?*

Ashley knew the answers to all those questions. We'd be sure to get them right. But what if Drew came up with a super-hard question that would stump us?

I glanced at Christina. She smiled back nervously. I checked my watch. The seconds ticked by so slowly! How long were we going to have to wait in here? I wondered.

Finally, the door opened, and Ashley, Billy, Marissa, and Matthew came in. I jumped up and hurried over to Ashley. "How did it go?" I whispered.

Ashley winked. "Easy!" she said. "We've got it *so* nailed. Don't worry about a thing."

Phew! I thought. That was good news!

Lauren came in behind them. "Everyone, put on your slime suits, because the green stuff's about to fly!" she cheered.

She opened a closet. Inside were the bright red plastic suits that we'd wear for the rest of the show. They were supposed to protect our clothes from the slime!

"The crew is going on break, so no one's allowed on the set," Lauren explained. "So you kids just relax. I'll let you know when it's time. And remember, no talking about your answers or you will be disqualified!"

Ashley and I grabbed two red suits from the closet. "I don't know about you," Ashley said as she pulled on the plastic top, "but I'm not getting *any* of that green stuff on me!"

I laughed. Ashley hated getting messy.

I heard an angry voice and looked across the room. Bobby was giving his brother a lecture. "I hope you didn't screw up!" Bobby pointed his finger in Billy's face.

Billy just stared at the floor. Suddenly he dropped his slime suit. His face turned green. "I'm going to be sick!" he called as he ran out of the room.

His brother groaned. Then he followed him out of the dressing room.

"Poor Billy," I whispered to Ashley.

"Yeah," Ashley agreed. "Can you imagine having a brother like Bobby?"

I shook my head. I couldn't imagine it. Ashley and I were competitive, but we always worked as a team.

Matthew and Christina put their suits on and wandered over to us.

"Ready to get slimed?" Matthew asked.

"Are you kidding?" I said. "I can't wait!"

"Unh-unh. Not going to happen," Ashley said confidently.

"Okay, twins! Time to go!" Lauren called to us. We all headed back to the set. When we got there, Kathy Goldbloom was already sitting behind her desk. She had a compact out and was checking her hair.

"Hey!" Ashley said. "She's not supposed to be here! How did she get out of the dressing room?"

"I don't know," I answered. "I didn't see her leave. Did you?"

Ashley shook her head.

As we all sat down, Billy and Bobby showed up. Billy still looked a little green.

Drew jumped onto the set and beamed into the camera. "Okay!" he said. "Time to see how well our twins know each other. We'll start with Billy and Bobby Branson."

Drew turned to the Branson twins. "The first question was 'What does your twin usually have for breakfast?' We asked Billy that question. Bobby, what do you think Billy said?"

"Easy," Bobby said. He glared at Billy. "I *always* have eggs and bacon for breakfast. *Always*."

Billy picked up a square piece of cardboard from his desk. He looked really nervous. His hands were shaking! But when he flipped his card over, it read EGGS AND BACON.

"That's right!" Drew said. "Ten points for the Branson twins."

"Yes!" Bobby cheered. He pumped his fist wildly in the air. Billy frowned. He slumped back into his seat.

Next up were the Goldblooms. Kathy shot us an icy smile. "Only the best for me and my sister," she said. "Buttermilk pancakes with fresh blueberries."

Marissa flipped over her card.

"Another right answer!" Drew said. "Ten points! How about the Martinez twins?"

Christina laughed nervously. "This is a tough one for us, Drew!" she admitted.

Matthew nodded. "Christina gets up really late. I never see what she has for breakfast!"

"I guess I usually have cereal in the morning," Christina said.

"Uh-oh." Matthew groaned. He flipped his card. It read FRUIT AND A GLASS OF ORANGE JUICE.

"Matthew," said Drew, "I'm afraid that's the wrong answer. You know what that means…"

Lights all over the set flashed, and a siren went off.

"*It's slime time!*" Drew yelled.

"Yaaah!" Matthew cried. Green goop dropped from the ceiling and poured down over his head.

"Yuck!" Christina said. She was splashed with slime, too.

Matthew smiled and wiped the goop out of his eyes. "Wow! That was awesome!"

"Now for the Trenchcoat Twins!" Drew turned to us. "Mary-Kate, what do you think Ashley said you eat most often for breakfast?"

"This is an easy one, Drew," I said. "I always have cereal for breakfast, usually cornflakes."

Ashley grinned. She picked up the card at the top of her stack and flipped it over.

"Oooh! I'm sorry, Mary-Kate," Drew said, "but Ashley answered that you like to have a chocolate doughnut for breakfast."

"Huh?" I said.

"What?" Ashley yelped at the same time.

I turned to my sister for an explanation. "That's not what I wrote!" she told me.

But it was too late. A siren blared. Lights flashed all over the set. The *Double Trouble* theme music kicked in, too. I heard a click from over our heads.

I looked up to see a wave of green slime coming right at us!

Sploosh! It poured down over Ashley's head.

Ashley sputtered and wiped at her face. "Wait! Stop the show!" She stood up. "Something's wrong! Someone switched our answers!"

4

THE CHEATER REPEATER

"**C**ut!" one of the cameramen yelled. The sirens wound down. The music stopped. All the lights stopped flashing.

Drew's bright smile turned into a deep frown. He walked over to our desk. "What's going on here, girls?" he asked us.

Ashley continued to wipe green slime off her face. "'Chocolate doughnuts' was not the answer I wrote down," she explained. "In fact, Mary-Kate doesn't even like chocolate doughnuts. She likes jelly doughnuts!"

"Are you saying that someone cheated?" Drew asked. "That's a very serious charge. Do you have any proof that someone switched your answers?"

"Well, no," Ashley admitted. "I just know that's not what I wrote on my card."

Drew shook his head. "Could it be that no one cheated and you're just upset about giving the wrong answer?"

"N-no!" Ashley started. "I—"

Drew sighed. "We see this all the time on *Double Trouble*. Some players just can't deal with losing. But I'm surprised at you, Ashley. I expected better sportsmanship from the Trenchcoat Twins."

Ashley's mouth dropped open. She sat back down in her seat. "I can't believe it!" she whispered. "He thinks I'm lying!"

The rest of the round went exactly the same way. The Bransons and Goldblooms got every answer right. The Martinezes missed a couple, but Ashley and I missed *every single question!* I couldn't believe it!

We were slimed so much that by the end of the round we looked like the Swamp Thing Twins!

After the last question there was a break. The cameras were turned off, and we all went backstage. Ashley and I grabbed our bags, then hurried to the bathroom to clean up.

Ashley was really mad. "Someone's cheating!" she said. "Every single one of my answers was changed!"

"It's crazy!" I agreed. "I mean, who would ever believe that my favorite animal at the zoo is a chicken? How lame!"

Ashley nodded. "It looks like we've got a mystery on our hands." She reached for her backpack and pulled out her detective notebook and a pencil.

"Hey! I didn't know you brought those!" I said.

Ashley grinned. "A good detective is

always prepared. You never know when you'll run into a mystery."

She opened the book and flipped to a blank page. "Okay. *Someone* changed our answers," she said. "The question is, who did it? And when did they do it?"

"Well, Drew Drewsdale made a big point of telling everyone that we were the team to beat," I said. "That means all of the other contestants are suspects."

"Right," Ashley agreed. She wrote the word "suspects" down in her notebook. Beneath that she printed the names of the other players.

I watched Ashley study the list. "But when did they do it? When would they have the chance to change the answers?" She pressed the tip of her pencil to her lips.

I thought hard about it. "Remember when we were changing into our slime suits? Lauren said the crew was on a break. There was no one on the set, so—"

"Someone could have sneaked over to the set and switched the answers when no one was looking!" Ashley finished my thought.

"In that case, it can't be the Martinez twins," I pointed out. "They were with us the whole time during the break. Besides, I can't believe they would cheat."

That left the Goldblooms and the Bransons.

"What about Bobby?" I asked. "He followed his brother out of the dressing room. Maybe he slipped over to the set while Billy was sick in the bathroom. Maybe he changed our answers."

"Hmmm. Bobby really does want to win," Ashley said. She underlined Bobby's name in her book. "What about Billy?" she asked.

I shook my head. "No way. He didn't look like he was feeling well. Besides, he seems like a nice guy. I don't think he would cheat."

Ashley nodded. "That's true. Okay, what

do you think about the Goldblooms?"

I snapped my fingers. "Hey, Kathy was already on the set when we got out there! I'm *sure* it was Kathy, Ashley! Let's go tell Drew!" I said.

"Wait a minute. Drew *already* doesn't believe us," Ashley pointed out. "Before we can accuse anybody, we need *proof*!"

"What about the answer cards?" I asked. "If somebody changed them, the answers should be in a different handwriting, right?"

"Wrong," Ashley said. "Whoever changed my answers did a really good job of matching my handwriting."

I sighed. "So we can't prove anything."

Ashley's eyes were sparkling. "Not *yet* we can't."

"I know that look," I told my sister. "You have a plan, don't you?"

THE BIG PLAN

Ashley nodded. "Here's the plan. Let's keep playing. You watch the Bransons. I'll watch the Goldblooms. If the cheater thinks we're not out to catch him, he's sure to strike again. And when he does, we'll be watching—"

"And waiting to pick up the clues and solve the case!" I finished. We slapped each other a high five. "Great plan, Ashley!"

"Let's go," my sister said. "And remember, keep your eyes open. We have to solve this mystery before the end of the show!"

We threw our backpacks over our shoulders and left the bathroom.

In the dressing room we ran into the rest of the contestants.

We dropped our bags in a corner. Kathy Goldbloom walked over to us, fluffing her goop-free hair. "We *told* you you'd lose," she said in a singsong voice. Her sister laughed.

"Yeah!" Bobby chimed in. "I guess I'm not so impressed with the Trenchcoat Twins after all!"

Billy hurried over to us when Bobby wasn't looking. "Gee, guys. I'm really sorry—"

"Billy!" Bobby snapped at him. "What did I tell you about making friends with the competition?"

"Well, I *am* sorry," Billy finished. He hung his head and walked back over to his brother.

There was a knock at the door. "Time for

Round Two!" Lauren called. "Everyone please make your way to the obstacle course set!"

"All right!" I cheered. For a second I forgot all about our mystery. On TV, the *Double Trouble* obstacle course always looked like so much fun! I couldn't wait to run it.

I was going to start the race. When I reached the halfway point, I would tag Ashley and she would finish the race. If either of us couldn't get over, around, under, or through an obstacle, we would wind up getting slimed!

We walked out to the set. "Okay, twins!" Drew called. "Let's get going!"

I walked up to the starting line. Bobby Branson, Matthew Martinez, and Marissa Goldbloom were there, too.

"Hey!" Bobby called out. "No fair! Mary-Kate and Ashley's lane is shorter!"

"What are you talking about?" I asked.

"Your lane is on the inside track," Bobby

said. "So it's shorter. I should know. I used to run track."

Drew rushed over to us. "What's the problem now?"

"My brother and I want to switch lanes with Mary-Kate and Ashley," Bobby told Drew.

Drew shook his head. For a moment, he seemed tired. "Mary-Kate, would you mind switching? I assure you, the lanes are exactly the same length."

I glanced over at Bobby. He had a sly grin on his face. He was definitely up to something. I'd have to keep a close watch on him.

"I don't mind," I said to Drew.

He smiled. "Thank you, Mary-Kate."

I took my place and focused on the course ahead of me. Ashley and I needed to win. We had no points from the first round!

Drew held up his hand. "Contestants," he said, "get on your marks…"

Bobby, Marissa, Matthew, and I moved forward.

"Get set…"

I bent my knees and got ready to run.

"Go!"

The four of us took off. I ran hard to the first obstacle, a long, low tunnel. I dove into the mouth of the tunnel and started crawling like crazy! When I got to the end, I jumped to my feet.

Without looking back, I sprinted to the next obstacle, a field of barrels. I dodged around the barrels at high speed.

Matthew and Marissa were way behind me, but Bobby was right on my tail!

I gritted my teeth and hopped through a bunch of tires. "Don't trip! Don't trip!" I told myself.

Yes! I cleared the last tire.

I charged up to my final obstacle. It was the hardest one! I had to climb a rope that hung over a pit of slime. Ashley was on a platform at the top of the rope, waiting.

"Come on, Mary-Kate!" she cheered.

Bobby and I jumped onto our ropes at the same time. I started to climb.

Hey! Something is wrong here, I thought. *This rope is slippery!*

I tried to hold on to the rope, but it was too greasy. And it smelled disgusting!

I've smelled that smell before, I realized. *But where?*

Before I could figure it out, my hands started to slip. I clung to the rope as tightly as I could. "Hold on! Hold on!" I told myself. But my hands started to slide.

"Helllllp!" I yelled as I fell down toward the pit of disgusting slime.

THE CHEATER "SLIPS" UP

*S*ploosh!

"Ugh!" I groaned. I was completely soaked in slime!

I waded over to the edge of the pit. When I reached the edge, I glanced up. Oh, no! Bobby was tagging his brother on top of the platform!

I looked for Marissa. She was halfway up her rope, and Matthew was jumping onto his. Everyone was passing us!

I leaped out of the pit. I grabbed the

rope in Billy and Bobby's lane. It wasn't greasy at all. I climbed up to the platform as fast as I could and tagged Ashley.

"Go! Go!" I cried.

Ashley took off. I watched as she swung down from the platform—like Tarzan! Her next obstacle was a set of monkey bars. She started swinging from bar to bar.

In the lane next to her, Christina zipped along the monkey bars. But the other twins were having trouble. Billy had already fallen from the monkey bars into the slime pit below. He was sloshing his way to the side.

I looked over at Kathy as she slowly swung from bar to bar. Her face was white with fright.

"Hey! It looks like your sister is going to win!" Matthew said to me.

Ashley had pulled ahead of Christina. She had only one obstacle left! She had to climb up a steep slide. At the top was the finish line—and first place!

Ashley started to climb her slide.

"Go, Ashley! Go!" I cheered.

Christina headed toward her slide and started to climb.

Ashley took another step—and her foot slid out from under her. She grabbed at the sides of the slide and pulled herself up.

She took another step—and slipped again!

"Oh, no!" she cried out as she slid down...down...down...and landed in a pit of slime with a loud *plop*.

"Come on, Ashley!" I cried. "Climb out!"

Ashley leaped out of the pit. She was dripping with green goop! She moved over to the next lane and tried to climb the slide there.

Ashley did it! She passed Christina and broke through the finish line!

"We won! We won!" I cried. Christina came in second. Billy and Kathy came in last.

Billy was stumbling, and he looked exhausted. His brother stormed up to him.

"If we lose this thing, it's going to be all your klutzy fault!" Bobby yelled.

Billy hung his head and started walking backstage. Bobby lectured him the whole way.

Ashley came up to me, and I gave her a hug. "Nice job!" I said.

"Thanks." She grinned.

Kathy and Marissa walked by us toward the dressing room. Kathy was touching her hair. She looked totally horrified—her hair had slime in it! "Is it bad?" she asked her sister. "Is it really bad?"

"Um..." Marissa bit her lip. "Well..."

"Oh, no!" Kathy said. "It's terrible, isn't it?" She covered her hair with her hands and hurried away.

"Congratulations, guys," Matthew and Christina said.

"You ran a tough race," Christina told Ashley.

"Thanks," Ashley said. "So did you!"

I turned to follow Christina and Matthew to the dressing room. But Ashley reached out and held me back.

"We need to talk," she said. "There was some kind of grease on the slide obstacle."

"There was something greasy on my rope, too!" I reported.

Ashley nodded. "Then someone definitely messed up our lane!"

"Wait a minute," I said. "That *wasn't* our lane! It was Billy and Bobby's. Until Bobby made us switch!"

"Good point." Ashley thought hard for a moment. "Do you think he asked to switch because he knew there was something wrong with his lane?"

"But how would he know that?" I paused. "Unless *Bobby* was the one who messed it up!"

"There's something else," Ashley said. "Did you notice anything interesting about the grease that was on your rope?"

"Yes!" I said. "It smelled really gross!"

Ashley nodded. "If we can figure out what smells like that, maybe we can figure out where the grease came from..."

"And who put it there," I finished.

Ashley and I walked over to the rope to study it. I rubbed my hand along it and took a whiff.

I wrinkled my nose. "I've got it!" I said. "It's Shine 'n' Soft hair gel. I can't stand that stuff!"

Ashley's face lit up. "You're right! Do you remember who was using Shine 'n' Soft back in the dressing room?"

"It was Kathy Goldbloom!" I said. "I knew it! Kathy is the cheater!"

"Hold on, Mary-Kate," Ashley said. "We've got to find the proof first."

Ashley and I headed for the dressing room and peeked inside.

"Good! No one is here," I said.

"Everyone must be in the bathroom,

cleaning off slime," Ashley said. "But we'd better hurry. They'll be back soon."

We found Kathy's bag sitting wide open in the far corner of the room. We started looking through it. Kathy had brought more hair products to the show than Ashley and I owned *together*. But…

"No Shine 'n' Soft." I sighed. "It's not here! Kathy must have gotten rid of the evidence!"

Ashley glanced around the room. "Wait a minute, Mary Kate," she said. She walked over to a blue bag across the room. She peeked inside.

"Bingo!" Ashley said. She pulled a half-full bottle of Shine 'n' Soft from the bag.

"It looks like someone else uses this hair gel," she told me. "And guess who it is!"

THE GEL TELLS ALL

"**W**hose bag is that?" I asked. "Who else uses Shine 'n' Soft gel?"

"Bobby Branson," Ashley replied. "This is his bag!"

I took the bottle from her and popped the top open. I took big whiff. "Yuck! That's the stuff on the rope all right!"

Ashley closed the bottle and put it back into Bobby's bag.

"So *Bobby* is the cheater!" I said. "It makes sense. He could have switched our cards during the break in Round One. And he has the gel."

"Plus, he asked us to switch lanes," Ashley pointed out.

"But wait a minute. What about Kathy?" I asked. "You and I both saw her using the Shine 'n' Soft earlier. Kathy could have stuck her bottle in Bobby's bag—to make it look like he did it!"

"You're right." Ashley frowned. "We can't say for sure if Kathy did it or if Bobby did. This is one tough case!"

"So what should we do now?" I asked.

"Let's play the last round and stick to the plan," Ashley said. "You keep an eye on Bobby. I'll watch Kathy. If someone slips up, we'll be there to catch him!"

"Or *her*," I reminded Ashley.

"Right," she said. "Let's go!"

Round Three, the final round, was a scavenger hunt. All four teams would be given a list of things to find. The more things we found, the more points we'd get.

Each team would be given a different amount of time on the hunt. Because Ashley and I had won the obstacle course, we got more time on the hunt. Since the Goldblooms came in last, they would be given the least amount of time.

Drew turned toward the camera when the game started again. "Hello, and welcome back!" he said. "We've tallied the scores from the first and second rounds. You'll be glad to know that it's anybody's game! This next round, the third and final, will determine our winner!"

I glanced around the set. Kathy and Marissa had done an amazing job in the bathroom. They were back to looking perfect. Plus, they didn't seem at all concerned that the game was so close.

Did they do something sneaky again? I wondered. Is that why they're so calm?

Bobby was giving Billy a pep talk. "When the going gets tough," he said, "the tough get going!"

Billy nodded and stared down at his brown shoes.

"Bobby sure does want to win badly," Ashley pointed out.

Christina and Matthew came over to us. "Ready for the last round?" Christina asked.

"Yup!" I said. "How about you?"

Christina nodded. She looked nervous. "It would be so great to win that computer!"

Matthew rubbed his hands together. "It sure would," he said.

We wished the Martinez twins luck.

"Thanks. And good luck to you guys, too," Matthew said.

Drew handed an envelope to each set of twins. Inside the envelope, we knew, was a list of the things we had to find.

"Is everybody ready?" Drew asked. "Remember, you can go anywhere you want on the set to find the items on your list."

The lights onstage grew brighter. Dramatic music began to play.

"Ready, Olsens? And...open 'em!" Drew shouted.

Ashley and I scrambled to open our envelope. Inside was a piece of paper with a short list.

"We'll be faster if we split up," Ashley suggested.

"Right," I said. I tore the list in two and gave one half to Ashley. "Good luck!" I called.

We raced off in separate directions. I looked down at my list. The first item was a hairbrush. Easy! I hurried backstage to our bags and grabbed my brush.

I glanced down at the list and read the next item: "Pen."

For a second, I panicked. Ashley and I hadn't brought a pen with us! We had a pencil and a notebook—but no pen!

Where can I get a pen? I wondered.

From Drew, I realized. He has one on his desk!

I spun around to race back out to the set and ran smack into Christina!

"Oof!" she said. "Sorry about that!"

"No problem," I told her. I hurried out to the set. Sure enough, there was a pen sitting on Drew's desk. I grabbed it. When I turned around, Christina was right behind me again!

"Hey," I said.

She smiled shakily. "Hey," she replied.

I hurried by her. I glanced at my list. My next item was "Key ring." Key ring? Where was I supposed to find a key ring?

I rushed backstage, not sure where to look. Lauren was there, watching over everyone. "Lauren," I said, running up to her. "You don't happen to have a key ring, do you?"

Lauren gave me a slow smile. "As a matter

of fact…" She reached into her pocket and pulled out a ring of keys. "But I need this back, okay?"

"Thanks!" I said. I grabbed them, spun around, ready to find the next item…and charged straight into Christina!

"You again?" I asked.

"Um, h-hey, Mary-Kate," Christina stammered.

This was getting too weird. "Christina, what are you doing?" I asked. "Are you following me?"

Christina looked shocked. "N-no, of course not." She backed away.

I shook my head. There was no time to worry about it now. I checked the next item on my list, "Bucket."

I figured I could find one in the janitor's closet!

After opening a few doors, I found a small room full of cleaning supplies.

Yes! Sitting on the floor, with a mop

inside it, was a shiny, silver bucket.

I darted inside. I reached for the bucket—and heard a *slam!*

Suddenly I was in total darkness.

Someone had closed the closet door!

"Hey!" I shouted. "I'm in here!"

I felt my way along the wall to the door. I groped for the doorknob. Found it.

I turned the knob.

Oh, no! The door was locked!

"Help!" I yelled. "Someone let me out. Hey—help!"

Then, in the darkness, I felt someone's hand on my shoulder....

"Aaaaaaaa!" I screamed.

8

TRAPPED!

"**A**aaaaaa!" I continued to shriek.

"Hey, hey, hey!" a boy's voice interrupted me. "Stop yelling. You're hurting my ears."

I spun around.

It was Bobby Martinez.

"Bobby? What are you doing in here?" I asked.

"Same as you," Bobby answered. "I'm looking for stuff. Who shut the door?"

"I don't know," I told him. "It's locked!"

Bobby shouldered past me and tried the

doorknob himself. "Oh, man! Someone locked us in here so we couldn't finish the scavenger hunt," he said. "That's cheating. Someone in this game is a cheater!"

"No kidding," I muttered.

"So your sister was telling the truth?" Bobby asked. "Someone really *did* switch your answers in Round One?"

"Ashley and I never lie," I told him.

We started banging on the door.

"Help!" we shouted together.

A moment later, the doorknob turned and the door swung open. It was Ashley!

"What happened?" she asked. Her arms were full of scavenger-hunt items.

"Later," Bobby called. "I have to make up for lost time!" He sprinted off.

"Someone locked us in," I explained. "Did you see anyone near this closet?"

Ashley frowned. "Yeah. I heard you guys calling. When I got here, Christina was running in the opposite direction."

"Christina," I repeated. "That's totally weird, because Christina has been following me the entire round!"

A loud bell rang, signaling the end of the round. I grabbed the bucket. Then Ashley and I ran out to the set.

Did Christina lock us in the janitor's closet? I wondered. Was she the cheater?

"That bell means time is up," Drew announced.

Ashley and I dumped our items on our desk. Lauren and some other people counted up everyone's points.

I glanced over at Christina. She wouldn't look at me.

"This is totally weird. The Martinezes have been so nice to us!" I whispered to my sister. "I can't believe they did it."

"They *do* want that computer really badly," Ashley reminded me.

"Yeah, I know," I said. "I just didn't think that they would cheat to get it."

The cameras were turned on, and Drew clapped his hands. "Your points have been tallied, and I'm happy to announce that the winners of today's special twins edition are...Christina and Matthew Martinez!"

"Yes!" Matthew cheered. Christina gave her brother a big hug.

"No fair!" Bobby shouted. "Someone cheated! Mary-Kate and I were locked in the janitor's closet. This show is rigged!"

Drew frowned, and once again the cameras were turned off. "Now *you're* telling me that someone is cheating?" Drew asked Bobby.

Bobby nodded. "That's right. Ask Mary-Kate. She was there. She'll back me up. We lost a lot of time."

"It's true," I told Drew. "Someone *did* lock me and Bobby in the closet."

Drew sighed. "This is terrible. Did either of you see who did it?"

I glanced over at Christina, but she still wouldn't look at me.

"No," I said.

Lauren and Drew talked quietly for a moment. Then Drew turned back to us. "We'll take a short break and then play the round over again."

We all filed backstage. Matthew and Christina were upset. I couldn't blame them. They'd just won the computer of their dreams, and it had been taken away.

Still, if they cheated to get it...

Ashley and I drifted off to talk to each other privately.

"Do you really think Christina and Matthew cheated?" I asked.

Ashley shook her head. "No. Christina may look suspicious, but she *couldn't* have cheated. She and Matthew have been hanging out with us almost the whole afternoon. They didn't have a chance to switch our answers in Round One. Or grease the obstacle course in Round Two."

"That's true," I said, relieved. "But Bobby can't be the cheater, either. He was trapped in the closet *with* me."

Ashley took her detective notebook out of her jeans pocket. She crossed Bobby Branson off the suspect list. "That means Kathy is the only suspect left," she reported.

"You're right," I agreed. "She slipped out of the dressing room during Round One. We saw her using Shine 'n' Soft hair gel—the same gel we found on the rope and the slide. Plus, she could have slammed the closet door."

I smiled. "I knew it was her! I knew it from the beginning."

Ashley nodded. "We need to set a trap to catch her in the act—to prove to everyone that Kathy is the cheater."

"But how?" I asked.

Ashley's eyes twinkled. "I have a plan. Come on, let's go talk to Drew."

9

THE TRAP IS SET!

A half hour later, Drew called all the contestants together on the set.

"Before we replay the final round," Drew said, "I have an announcement to make. *I know who the cheater is.*"

Everybody gasped.

"You mean someone really is cheating?" Kathy Goldbloom asked.

I narrowed my eyes at her. *As if you didn't know,* I thought.

"Yes. It's all true," Drew said.

"How did you figure out who did it?" Ashley asked.

"Evidence!" Drew told her. "I have plenty of evidence pointing to one person. And it's all in my dressing room."

"Who is it?" I asked.

"Yeah," Bobby said. "Who's the worm that locked me in the closet?"

Drew shook his head. "I'm not going to announce that until after the show is over. Now, let's replay the final round!"

I looked at the other contestants. Bobby was busy giving Billy a final pep talk. "This is it!" he was saying. "We really have to go for it this time!"

Billy's shoulders slumped as he listened.

Christina and Matthew looked tense, but who could blame them? They had to win that computer all over again.

The Goldblooms huddled in a corner, whispering and frowning.

Ah-ha! I thought. Marissa and Kathy

know we're on to them, and now they're worried.

I smiled to myself. The trap was set, and soon Kathy Goldbloom would fall right into it!

Each team of twins was handed a new scavenger-hunt envelope. It had a different list of objects inside. When Drew said "Go!" Ashley and I opened ours.

"We're staying together this time, right?" Ashley asked.

"Right," I said, giving her a thumbs-up.

We looked at the first item on our list, "Gorilla mask."

"A gorilla mask? Where do we find one of those?" Ashley asked.

"Maybe there's a costume room around here," I guessed. "Let's go!"

Ashley and I ran backstage to look for a costume room. Soon the other contestants were zipping around on their own searches.

Next to our dressing room, we found a

closet full of masks and costumes! All right!

Ashley and I charged inside. We searched through cartons that lined the floor.

"I found it!" Ashley cried. "I found the—"

CRASH!

We both turned to the door.

"It worked!" I cheered. "Our trap worked! We caught Kathy!"

We ran out of the costume room and down the hall to Drew's dressing room.

There, lying on the floor, was someone totally covered with slime.

"Awesome! We caught her!" Ashley crowed.

"Who?" a girl's voice asked. "Who did you catch?"

We turned around. Standing behind us was—Kathy Goldbloom!

Huh?

"If that's not Kathy under the slime," I said, "then who is it?"

THE CHEATER REVEALED

The slimed person sputtered, coughed, and wiped the slime off his face.

It was…Billy Branson!

Ashley and I gasped.

"Billy?" Ashley asked.

"No way!" I said. "I don't believe it!"

By then, the rest of the contestants had heard the noise. They gathered in a crowd behind us. Drew and Lauren were there, too.

"Mary-Kate, Ashley, did our trap work?" Drew asked. "Did we catch the cheater?"

"Yeah," I answered sadly. "We caught him."

Billy seemed like such a nice guy. How could he be the cheater? I wondered.

"What do you mean, 'our trap'?" Marissa asked.

"Drew helped us," Ashley explained. "We figured the cheater would come here and try to steal the evidence against him. So we set up a huge bucket of slime to drop on the next person who walked through Drew's door."

"But we never thought it would turn out to be Billy," I said.

"Billy?" Bobby's voice called from the back of the group. "What do you mean, Billy?" He pushed his way to the front. His mouth hung open when he saw his brother lying on the floor in a puddle of goo.

"You?" Bobby asked. "*You're* the cheater?"

Billy nodded. "Yes. It was me all along."

"But why?" Ashley asked. "Why would you do that to me and Mary-Kate? You didn't seem to want to win at all!"

Billy glared at his brother. "You're right. I didn't want to win. I cheated because I wanted to be sure that Bobby and I lost!"

"*What?*" Bobby shouted.

"You're so mean to everybody!" Billy told his brother. "And you want to win all the time. I thought you deserved to lose."

Bobby stood there—speechless. His face began to turn red.

"I'm confused, Billy," I said. "If you were trying to make sure *you* lost, why did *our* stuff keep getting messed up?"

Billy blushed. "I goofed," he said. "In the first round, I wanted to change my answers, but I changed yours by accident. Then I greased up our lane in the obstacle course, but Bobby changed lanes with you. And when I locked Bobby in the closet, I didn't realize you were in there, too!"

"Wow!" Ashley whispered to me.

I turned to Christina. "I don't understand something," I said to her. "Why were you following me around during the scavenger hunt?"

Now it was Christina's turn to look embarrassed. "I really wanted that computer," she said. "I figured if anyone knew how to find the stuff on our lists, it would be a great detective like you. I'm sorry, Mary-Kate."

I smiled. "That's all right," I said.

"I'm sorry, too," Drew said. "I'm sorry that we're going to have to disqualify Billy and Bobby from the game."

I looked at Bobby. I expected him to explode. But instead he just looked sad.

"Gee, Billy," he said. "I guess I didn't realize how crazy I was about winning. I'm sorry."

Billy nodded. He pulled a tissue from his jeans to wipe off his goop-covered glasses.

Bobby held out his hand to help up his brother.

"Aw, isn't that sweet?" Kathy Goldbloom said in a nasty tone. "Now let's get to the important part—*who won*?"

Drew glanced down at a piece of paper in his hand. "Let me see. This is complicated." He scratched his head. "First we have to finish this scavenger hunt do-over."

I glanced over at Ashley. She smiled. We both knew what we wanted to do.

"Let's use the scores from the first hunt, Drew," I suggested.

"In that case, our winners are *still* Christina and Matthew Martinez!" Drew announced.

"All right!" Christina and Matthew cheered. Ashley and I gave them both a hug. We were so happy for them!

"Hmmph. We didn't want to win anyway," Kathy and Marissa said. They fluffed their perfect hair and walked off.

We were all about to follow them, when Drew stopped us.

"Hold on, gang," Drew said. "Don't you want to know who won second prize?"

We all stopped. "Sure," Ashley said.

"Why not?" I agreed.

"Ladies and gentlemen, the second prize winners are...Mary-Kate and Ashley Olsen!" Drew shouted.

"Hooray, Trenchcoat Twins!" Matthew and Christina cheered.

"What do we win?" I asked Drew.

"Well, it's not as nice as a new computer," he admitted.

"That's okay," Ashley said. "Tell us!"

"The second-prize winners receive a year's supply of Soft 'n' Shine hair gel and a bucket of Double Trouble slime to play with at home!"

Ashley and I looked at each other, and we burst out laughing. "I can't believe it!" Ashley giggled.

"Neither can I!" I replied. "Total yuck!"

"Well," Drew said, "shall we go tape the end of the show? I need to announce the winners on camera."

"Let's do it!" Christina cheered.

Ashley and I followed Drew out to the set. I slung my arm around my sister's shoulders. "You know, even if we didn't come in first, I already feel like a winner," I told her.

"Really? How come?" Ashley asked.

I grinned. "Because solving mysteries with someone you love is the best prize in the whole world!"

Hi from both of us,

We were excited to watch our friend, Patty O'Leary, dance in the International Talent Show at the mall. But at dance practice, someone stole Patty's lucky four-leaf-clover diamond pin!

After that, jewelry started disappearing all over the mall. And it was up to Ashley and me to find out who was behind the crimes!

Want to find out more? Turn the page for a sneak peek at our latest case, *The New Adventures of Mary-Kate & Ashley: The Case of the Mall Mystery.*

See you next time!

The New Adventures of MARY-KATE & ASHLEY

A sneak peek at our next mystery...

The Case Of The

Mall Mystery

"How can I do an Irish jig, if I don't have my shamrock?" our friend, Patty O'Leary cried.

My sister, Ashley, and I were standing in front of a stage in the center of the mall. In a few minutes, Patty was supposed to dance in the International Talent Show.

But we were in the middle of a mystery! Someone had stolen Patty's diamond shamrock pin.

"Don't worry, Patty. We have a plan to catch the jewelry thief," I said.

Ashley held up a bag that said SPARKLE JEWELRY on it. "We put some of our own jewelry in this bag," she explained. "I'm going to walk around the mall with it. Meanwhile Mary-Kate's going to keep a close eye on me."

I nodded. "That way, when the jewelry thief tries to snatch the bag, we'll catch him in the act!"

Patty smoothed down her green velvet dress. "I hope it works," she said. "I need that pin back now!"

Ashley turned to me. "Ready?" she asked.

I gave her a thumbs-up. "Ready. Good luck, Ashley!"

My sister strolled around the center of the mall.

I hid near the stage, behind a cutout of the Eiffel Tower, and watched as she passed all the cool carts nearby.

There were people shopping at the Fancy Flowers cart, the Sparkle Jewelry cart, the Totally T-shirts cart, and the

Chocolates Galore cart. But no one looked very suspicious.

Then the lights in the mall dimmed. The show was about to begin!

"Ladies and gentlemen," a booming voice announced. "Welcome to our International Talent Show!"

Colorful spotlights shone on the stage. Ashley stopped. She put the jewelry bag down at her feet. Then she gave me a quick wink.

I shivered with excitement. I was sure the thief would grab that bag. And when he did, I'd be ready!

"For our first act," the announcer continued. "Please welcome Michael Santino— the dancing Tower of Pisa!"

Michael climbed onstage, dressed as a huge tower. He threw his arms up and swayed left and right.

I glanced back down at the bag. It was still there. It hadn't even moved an inch.

Next a girl wearing a kimono performed. Then a boy in a sombrero did a Mexican hat dance.

The jewelry bag stayed exactly where Ashley had put it.

Then a tall blond girl walked onto the stage. She cupped her hands around her mouth.

"Yodele-he-hooooooo!" She let out the loudest yodel I've ever heard!

"Eeek!" I shut my eyes and covered my ears. That yodeling hurt my eardrums!

I opened my eyes again and glanced over at Ashley's feet to check on the Sparkle Jewelry bag.

Oh, no! My mouth dropped open. I couldn't believe it. I had only taken my eyes off the bag for a second.

But it was gone. The thief had struck again!

Reading Checklist
ndashley
ngle one!

☐ It's a Twin Thing
☐ How to Flunk Your First Date
☐ The Sleepover Secret
☐ One Twin Too Many
☐ To Snoop or Not to Snoop?
☐ My Sister the Supermodel
☐ Two's a Crowd
☐ Let's Party!
☐ Calling All Boys
☐ Winner Take All
☐ P. S. Wish You Were Here
☐ The Cool Club
☐ War of the Wardrobes
☐ Bye-Bye Boyfriend

☐ It's Snow Problem
☐ Likes Me, Likes Me Not
☐ Shore Thing
☐ Two for the Road
☐ Surprise, Surprise
☐ Sealed With A Kiss

Super Specials:
☐ My Mary-Kate & Ashley Diary
☐ Our Story
☐ Passport to Paris Scrapbook
☐ Be My Valentine

**Available wherever books are sold,
or call 1-800-331-3761 to order.**